Ho for a Hat!

By William Jay Smith
Illustrated by Lynn Munsinger

Little, Brown and Company
BOSTON TORONTO LONDON

Text copyright © 1964, 1989 by William Jay Smith
Illustrations copyright © 1989 by Lynn Munsinger

All rights reserved. No part of this book may
be reproduced in any form or by any electronic or
mechanical means, including information storage
and retrieval systems, without permission in
writing from the publisher, except by a reviewer
who may quote brief passages in a review.

First Paperback Edition

Library of Congress Cataloging-in-Publication Data

Smith, William Jay, 1918–
Ho for a hat! / written by William Jay Smith; illustrated by Lynn Munsinger.
p. cm.
Summary: A young boy and his dog observe and try on a variety of hats.
ISBN 0-316-80120-8 (hc)
ISBN 0-316-80126-7 (pb)
[1. Hats—Fiction. 2. Stories in rhyme.] I. Munsinger, Lynn, ill. II. Title.
PZ8.3.S6712Ho 1989
[E]—dc19 88-39864

Joy Street Books are published by
Little, Brown and Company (Inc.)

10 9 8 7 6 5 4 3 2 1

BP

Published simultaneously in Canada
by Little, Brown & Company (Canada) Limited

Printed in the United States of America

For Alexandre in his many hats

— W. J. S.

For Hannah

— L. M.

Round or square
Or tall or flat,
People love
To wear a Hat.

Ho for a Hat
To put on your head!

A Hat tall and black
A Hat round and red
A tall Hat
A small Hat
A plumed Hat
A square Hat
A straw Hat
A bear Hat

A Hat like a stovepipe
A Hat like a pot

A Hat you fold up

A Hat you cannot

A Hat to put on to keep off the sun,
A Hat to take off when work is all done.

A Hat to wear cocked on the side of your head,
To throw in the air,
To toss on the bed

To doff to the ladies
To fling on a chair

To hang on a hook
To have and to wear
To have and to carry
To have and to hold

A Hat black as night

A Hat bright as gold!

A Hat that can sit on your head
Just like that.

Ho for a Hat!

Hats are pretty,
Hats are fun,
Rain Hats for rain

Straw Hats for sun.

They look nice,

They feel nice,

They *are* nice,

And *that's*
The reason for Hats!

The cowboy in his broad-brimmed Hat
Ropes a steer with his lariat,
Then rides away.

Hats are for work

Hats are for play.

Silk or wool,
Straw or tin,
Round as an orange,
Thin as a pin,

Flat as a pancake,
Tall as a stack,
Furnace-red,
Midnight-black.

Hats are handsome,
Hats are fun,

Hats are magic.

Look at this one
The Magician wears.
He takes it off,
And what comes out?

An egg

A rabbit

A flock of doves.

Out they fly and up goes a shout —
And that is that!

Ho for a Hat!

People wear Hats in the shape of bells,
Towers, pagodas, cabbages, shells,
Hats made of velvet,
Hats made of silk,

Hats like plates
Or bottles of milk.

Hats like sailboats under sail,
Hats topped with flowers, draped with veil
That covers the face
In spidery lace . . .

And Hats that have come
From outer space. . . .

Let's take all the Hats
That can be found
Hats that are square
Hats that are round.
A Hat that's nice to wear — O
A bright new sombrero —

Let's take them all
Large and small
Tall or flat
Round or square,

And carry them all to the top of the stair
And throw them all up high in the air
To the people gathered round about
While you and I together shout:

Ho for a Hat!